# Alan

# Burke

**Stories shared by Alan and Burke - passed on from one generation to another**

# Contents

# CONTRIBUTORS

Written by **Humairah Shah**

Illustrated by **Javier C Gonzalez**

Cover and book design by **Shah Faisal**

# Sam and the Sugar Bug

Written by: Dr. Humairah Shah
Illustrations by: Javier C Gonzalez III

Leila had been taking good care of her teeth. She would always brush her teeth in the morning and at night before going to bed. Leila's brother, Sam, would sometimes get lazy and forget to brush his teeth, especially at night.

One night, Sam had dinner and went to sleep without brushing his teeth. Randy, the evil sugar bug, was looking for food and was very hungry. Randy snuck into Leila's room and found nothing. Randy went from room to room looking for food, until at last he entered Sam's room.

"I smell food," said Randy, with an evil grin.

Evil Randy followed the scent and it led him to Sam's mouth. Randy jumped into Sam's mouth and said, "I am going to have a feast tonight! There is lot of food sticking to these teeth!" Randy had dinner and now he was full of energy. He decided that he would stay in Sam's mouth. Now he did not have to go looking for food every night. Randy started building his new home in Sam's teeth.

In the morning, Sam brushed his teeth in a hurry. If Sam had brushed long enough, he might have been able to kick evil Randy out of his mouth. Now Randy had more time to work on building his home in Sam's mouth and he grew stronger and stronger with all the food he was getting.

9

One night, after Sam fell asleep, Randy invited his friends to his home. They had a big party in Sam's mouth. Suddenly, Sam's tooth began to hurt. Sam woke up in pain.

"Mommy, my mouth hurts," Sam cried.

Poor Sam was up all night. The next day, Sam's mom took him to Dr. Jane.

11

Dr. Jane looked at Sam's teeth with her magic mirror and was upset with what she saw. Randy and his friends were playing in Sam's teeth. Dr. Jane told Sam and his mother what she had found.

"That is why your teeth hurt," explained Dr. Jane.

"I will clean your teeth and get rid of Randy and his friends," said Dr. Jane. She used her magic whistle to spray lot of water into Sam's mouth. The sugar bugs felt the house shake and soon it was full of water. Randy and his friends were scared and had no idea what was happening.

They tried to escape but Dr. Jane and Suzie, the nurse, were quick to catch them. They found them hiding in the corner of the house. One by one, Dr. Jane and Suzie got rid of all the bugs. Dr. Jane fixed and filled all the holes that naughty Randy had dug in Sam's teeth.

Sam was happy that Randy and his friends no longer lived in his mouth. From that day on, he always brushed his teeth long enough to remove all the food. Sam brushed for two minutes every morning and every night, and he never let sugar bugs get into his mouth again.

*Stop it! You guys are making my life hard.*

**- Randy**

# Leila Visits the Dentist

Written by: Dr. Humairah Shah
Illustrations by: Javier C Gonzalez III

Leila was going to see the dentist.

"What is a dentist, mommy?" asked Leila.

"A dentist takes care of your teeth and makes sure they are nice and strong. The dentist also makes sure that no sugar bugs live in your mouth," explained Leila's mom.

At the dentist's office, there were other kids and parents too.

After a while, Susie, the nurse, took Leila and her mom to a room. It was a beautiful room and it reminded Leila of the zoo. There were colorful pictures of animals all around.

"Leila, I have to take some pictures of your teeth," said Susie.

Susie showed Leila the camera. It was a big blue camera, much bigger than the one Leila had at home.

Leila sat on a chair and Susie placed an apron with a big happy face on her. Leila took lot of pictures with the giraffe, bear and monkey.

"I am going to get your pictures ready and in the meantime, you can watch a movie," said Suzie.

"This place is fun," said Leila.

After a while, Susie took Leila to see Dr. Jane. Dr. Jane had Leila lie down on a chair. She had a magic mirror and a special tooth counter.

"I have to count your teeth and see if you have any sugar bugs in them," said Dr. Jane.

Leila opened her mouth big and wide like an alligator so Dr. Jane could have a good look at her teeth.

Dr. Jane looked for bugs with her magic mirror and counted them with the tooth counter. When she was done, she had a big smile on her face.

"Leila, you have twenty teeth and they are pretty clean and strong. There are no sugar bugs in your mouth," said Dr. Jane.

Dr. Jane reminded Leila that she had to brush her teeth for two minutes every morning and every night. She suggested Leila listen to her favorite song and brush from the time it starts till it ends.

"Do not forget to floss at night as well; sugar bugs love to hide between your teeth," said Dr. Jane.

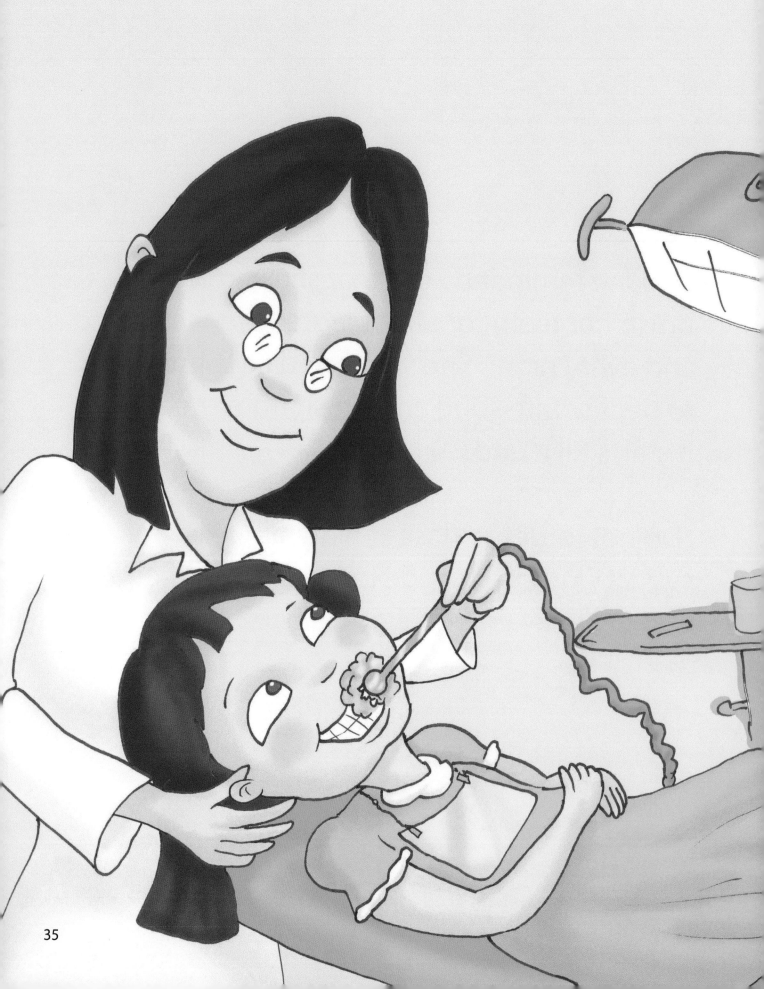

"Leila, I am going to brush your teeth now," explained Dr. Jane.

"Dr. Jane that toothbrush looks different," pointed out Leila.

"Yes it is. It's a very special toothbrush. It goes round and round and makes a zzzzzzzz sound. Would you like the cherry or strawberry flavored toothpaste?" asked Dr. Jane.

"Cherry is my favorite," said Leila happily.

So Dr. Jane brushed Leila's teeth with the cherry toothpaste.

Dr. Jane's tooth brush was funny. It tickled Leila's teeth and made her laugh. Now that Leila was done, she got to pick two toys and a tooth brush.

"I love this place mommy and the dentist too! I want to come back and see Dr. Jane again," said Leila.

"Oh yes, we certainly will," said her mother.

Make sure you visit your dentist every six months after your first birthday. Remember, no rushing when brushing.

- Alan and Burke

*I hate Alan and Burke.*

**- Randy**

*Thank you for taking the time to read this book. If your child enjoyed the book, please write a 5-star review on Amazon today. That would be greatly appreciated!*

- Humairah Shah

Printed in Great Britain
by Amazon

82916595R00027